Dear Parent:
Your child's love of reading starts here!

Every child learns to read in a different way and at his or her own speed. Some go back and forth between reading levels and read favorite books again and again. Others read through each level in order. You can help your young reader improve and become more confident by encouraging his or her own interests and abilities. From books your child reads with you to the first books he or she reads alone, there are I Can Read Books for every stage of reading:

SHARED READING
Basic language, word repetition, and whimsical illustrations, ideal for sharing with your emergent reader

BEGINNING READING
Short sentences, familiar words, and simple concepts for children eager to read on their own

READING WITH HELP
Engaging stories, longer sentences, and language play for developing readers

READING ALONE
Complex plots, challenging vocabulary, and high-interest topics for the independent reader

ADVANCED READING
Short paragraphs, chapters, and exciting themes for the perfect bridge to chapter books

I Can Read Books have introduced children to the joy of reading since 1957. Featuring award-winning authors and illustrators and a fabulous cast of beloved characters, I Can Read Books set the standard for beginning readers.

A lifetime of discovery begins with the magical words "I Can Read!"

Visit www.icanread.com for information
on enriching your child's reading experience.

For Eli
—B.L.

To Del Preston,
with appreciation
—T.B.

HarperCollins®, ☙®, and I Can Read Book® are trademarks of HarperCollins Publishers Inc.

Library of Congress Cataloging-in-Publication Data is available.
ISBN-10: 0-06-073687-9 (trade bdg.) — ISBN-13: 978-0-06-073687-3 (trade bdg.)
ISBN-10: 0-06-073688-7 (lib. bdg.) — ISBN-13: 978-0-06-073688-0 (lib. bdg.)

1 2 3 4 5 6 7 8 9 10 ❖   First Edition

Custard Surprise

By Bernard Lodge
Pictures by Tim Bowers

HarperCollins*Publishers*

Early one morning, Dinah and Rufus

opened a restaurant.

They called it Dinah's Diner.

"I'll look after the customers,"

said Dinah.

"And I'll do the cooking,"

said Rufus.

Rufus cooked beanburgers,
carrot crumble, peanut pancakes,
and a yummy dessert.

"Just wait till they try

my Custard Surprise," said Rufus.

"It's so tasty! I've made buckets of it."

But no one came for breakfast.

In fact, no one came for hours.

"Isn't anybody hungry?"

asked Rufus.

Just then, a hungry mule walked in.

"Welcome to Dinah's Diner,"

said Dinah.

"We've got beanburgers,

carrot crumble, peanut pancakes,

and best of all, our dish of the day—

Custard Surprise!"

"What? No hay?" asked the mule.

"I don't know," said Dinah.

"Let me ask the cook."

"Hay?" yelled Rufus. "This is a diner, not a farmyard!"

But he climbed on the roof

and hacked off some straw.

"Hay or straw, what's the difference?"

said Rufus.

"The mule won't know."

13

Rufus was so mad

that he wobbled off his ladder.

"No broken bones," said Dinah,
fixing his wing in a sling.

Then Rufus made a straw salad

with olives and ketchup.

He spiced it up with red chili peppers.

"Super!" said the mule.

"Hottest hay I ever tasted!"

At noon, a hungry crow flew in.

"Welcome to Dinah's Diner,"
said Dinah.

"We've got beanburgers,
carrot crumble, peanut pancakes,
and best of all, our dish of the day—
Custard Surprise!"

"What? No worms?" asked the crow.

"I don't know," said Dinah.

"Let me ask the cook."

"Worms?" yelled Rufus.

"Yuck! I gave them up years ago. But how about some spaghetti cut into worm-size bits?"

"Now, to make the spaghetti pink, I'll add a drop of jam and . . . oops!"

The jam spilled out of the jar—
and all over Rufus!

"Fantastic!" said the crow.

"Sweetest worms I ever tasted."

The next guest was a hungry bear.

"Welcome to Dinah's Diner,"

said Dinah.

"We've got beanburgers,

carrot crumble, peanut pancakes,

and best of all, our dish of the day—

Custard Surprise!"

"What? No honey?" asked the bear.

"I don't know," said Dinah.

"Let me ask the cook."

"Honey?" yelled Rufus.

"We don't have any honey."

"So borrow some
from the bees next door!"
begged Dinah.

"Good idea!" said Rufus.

But the bees didn't think so.

"Only a couple of stings,"
said Dinah, patching him up.

"Forget the honey!" said Rufus.

"I'll use mustard and add syrup

to make it sweet."

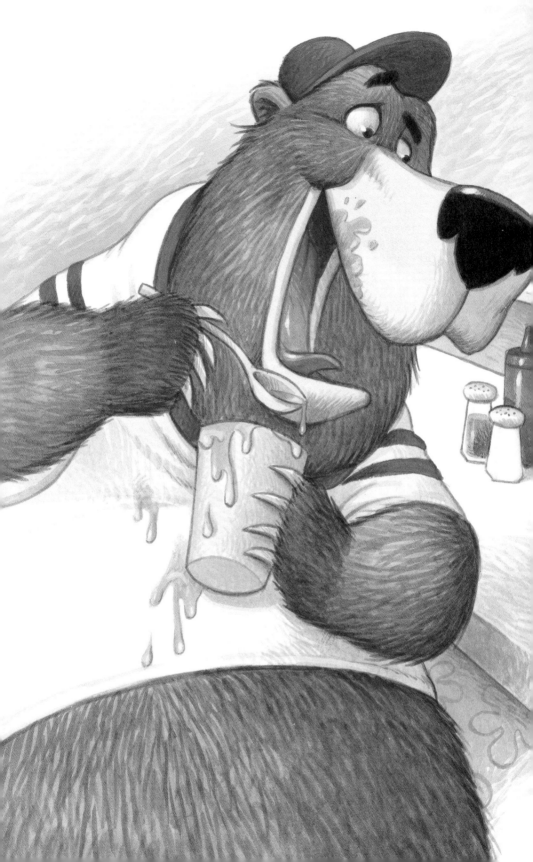

"Yummy!" said the bear.

"Nicest honey I ever tasted."

Before long, a hungry goat stopped by.
"Welcome to Dinah's Diner,"
said Dinah.

"We've got beanburgers,

carrot crumble, peanut pancakes,

and best of all, our dish of the day—

Custard Surprise!"

The goat grabbed the menu.

"Great!" he said.

"Crunchiest menu I ever tasted."

Dinah ran to the kitchen.

"There's a goat out there

eating the menu!" she cried.

"So what?" growled Rufus.

"I don't care if he eats
the tablecloth, too.
Nobody wants my Custard Surprise."

The last customer of the day
was a very hungry fox.

"Welcome to Dinah's Diner,"
said Dinah.

"We've got beanburgers,
carrot crumble, peanut pancakes,
and best of all, our dish of the day—
Custard Surprise!"

"Maybe for dessert," said the fox.

"But first, I'd like something meaty . . .

like a plump, juicy chicken!"

He leaped over the counter

and chased Dinah

right into the kitchen.

Well, Dinah was plump,

but she wasn't slow.

She gave the fox the surprise

of his life—a CUSTARD SURPRISE!

The fox never came back.

The other animals made sure of that.

They loved Dinah's Diner,

and they wanted to eat there again.

"There's some Custard Surprise
left over," said Dinah.
"It would be a pity to waste it."
"Yes," said Rufus. "And you know,
it's really quite good."

"*Mmmmm,*" said the fox.

"Best custard I ever tasted."